Mom's New Friend

Written and Illustrated by Mattia Cerato

RED
CHAIR
·PRESS·

Please visit our website at www.redchairpress.com.
Find a free catalog of all our high-quality products for young readers.

Mom's New Friend

Publisher's Cataloging-In-Publication Data
(Prepared by The Donohue Group, Inc.)

Cerato, Mattia.

Mom's new friend / written and illustrated by Mattia Cerato.
p. : col. ill. ; cm. -- (Family snaps)
Summary: A young boy is reluctant to accept his mom's new friend, Dan. However, when they all go on a road trip together, he finds that Dan is not as bad as he imagined.
Interest age level: 005-008.
Issued also as an ebook.
ISBN: 978-1-936163-96-0 (lib. binding/hardcover)
ISBN: 978-1-939656-61-2 (pbk.)
ISBN: 978 1-936163-97-7 (eBk)
1. Children of single parents--Juvenile fiction. 2. Man-woman relationships--Juvenile fiction. 3. Dating (Social customs)--Juvenile fiction. 4. Automobile travel--Juvenile fiction. 5. Single mothers--Fiction. 6. Man-woman relationships--Fiction. 7. Dating (Social customs)--Fiction. 8. Automobile travel--Fiction. I. Title.
PZ7.C472 Mo 2014

[E]   2013956104

First published by:
Red Chair Press LLC   PO Box 333   South Egremont, MA 01258-0333

Printed in the United States of America

1 2 3 4 5 18 17 16 15 14

Mom's got a new friend.

I haven't met him yet. But I don't think I'll like him.

Mom says on Sunday we will go on a trip with him.

Her new friend is named Dan.

There's a boy at school that stinks a lot called Dan.

They say he's never showered in his whole life.

I don't like leaving home.

I can play video games when I'm home.

But I can't if we leave on Sunday.

Mom says we'll see lots of **animals.**
I like animals, but I can read about them at home.

Mom says that Dan has a big **Car**.
It can drive in mud and across rivers.

She says the trip will be **fun.**

To me, it just looks **dirty**.

Maybe it's dirty **and** stinky
like the Dan at my school.

Are we there yet?

Mom says you have to be patient to see the beautiful sights. But I know they will be ugly and boring. I'd rather be home.

Why can't I stay in the car?

Mom says we have to hike now to reach the waterfall.
I don't want to hike just to see some boring water.

Mom says we'll see some cool sights on the way.

What kind of animal is that?

"It's called a wombat," says Dan.

He looks sad. I wonder why.
"Maybe he's sad because he lives by **himself**,"
Dan answers.

Dan tells me to look above. There's a koala on the tree.
She looks lost.

Does she live alone too?

"She's only **hungry**," says Dan.
"Her friend has brought her food now.

She looks much **happier,** don't you think?"

Maybe Dan is right.

A snake! **Snakes are scary. What now?**

"Don't worry," says Dan. "He's just showing off for his friend. He must be in love with her."

Oh no, Spiders, too!

"Don't be afraid" says Dan.
"He won't harm us.
He's building a web for
his new **family.**"

Finally, we get to the **Waterfall.**

Wow! I have never been to such a beautiful place.
It's not the same as on TV or in a book.

I guess I liked hiking

through the woods and seeing all the animals. Maybe we can go back sometime.

"Of course," says Mom. "Dan will show us a lot of new places."

I guess Dan is okay.

Anyway, Mom says he'll be
coming around a lot now.

Dan tells me he **likes** video games.
Now when he's here, we play together a lot.

I'm pretty sure he'll **never** beat me though.

Dan spends a lot of time with us now.

He really is okay. Maybe more than okay.

And... he doesn't **stink!**